"Will you please get up and help with our son?" My wife was frustrated and I was dead tired. I had slept, but the dream seemed so real, that I wondered if I rested. "And don't forget Sunday is November 1st, All Saints Day, we are supposed to go to church with your Grandma." The urgency hit me and I jumped out of bed. I realized I only had two more days, or I would have to wait another year.

"Where is Silas?"

"In his room, still in his pajamas."

"I'll get him dressed and drop him off at the daycare on my way to work."

"You are such a dear." My wife leaned over and kissed my forehead as I was sitting on the edge of the bed, wrestling with long pants. The chill of fall was turning the leaves bitter shades of orange and brown.

"There he is." Silas reached up with his tiny arms and pulled his open mouth to my cheek in an awkward attempt to kiss it. Bundling him in warm clothes I dashed out the door with him in the crook of my arm, strapping him into the car seat in the back of my worn and rusty Volvo.

'It's that spooky time of the year! Are you folks ready to get down with the *undead*?' I reached over and turned down the radio, snatching a look to the back seat, Silas' head was turned watching the scenery flow by.

Don't forget to pay for the daycare this week.

My wife's voice tended to float into my mind like a disembodied head, reminding me of something I had forgotten and would probably forget again.

Silas was very social, he launched himself into the playroom with the other kids, all of them teetering between baby and full-on toddlers. I smiled realizing how truly blessed I was to have him and Carol. Even as happy as I was I couldn't get Andrea out of my mind. *Let go of the past honey.* Carol's voice again. Andrea's love scarred my soul. Her memories burdened my mind.

Waving at my mates in the office, I shut the door to mine and fumbled around at the desk for the book. Turning to a familiar worn page in the Book of the Dead, I recited the prayer.

On All Hallow's Eve, after midnight the dead will wake. Cross the River Styx and best the guardian to reunite with the dead. Touch the river and be consumed by madness. Touch the guardian be stricken with the disease. Consumed by the beast, die in your sleep.

Dia de Morte, Dia de Morte, Dia de Morte....

I started the chant in my mind and lay my head down on the book. Within seconds, the fabric of the real world splintered and I entered the barren landscape that I had been running through, night after night.

Tortured, twisted, colorless trees flashed by. My heart was lurching in my chest before the howl shattered the silence. They were on my trail again, hideous four-legged monsters that outweighed me by a hundred pounds. They had crushed me night after night before I could even reach the river. Last night I caught a glimpse of the river, just as I was overrun.

Andrea appeared in my thoughts and smiled. Looking over, a sapphire staff was leaning on a rock. I grabbed the staff and turned, standing my ground. Pointing the staff, a river of energy burst from the end of it incinerating the lead creature of the pack. The rest of them snarled and gnashed their teeth, pacing back and forth, none willing to test me with my new weapon. I tapped the butt of the staff on the ground and scintillating blue lightning crackled and popped from it, sending tremors through the ground. The beasts howled in unison, turned, and evaporated back into the gray of the woods.

Turning and walking I could see the edge of the river, its liquid the color of obsidian, its lack of movement deceiving. The guards of the woods were nothing compared to the leviathan. The Book of the Dead didn't describe it, only saying just a glimpse of it had the power to destroy a person's mind.

Keeping a safe distance from the edge, I watched and waited. Andrea's face appeared again in my thoughts. Her mouth slowly churned as ripples disturbed the surface of the River Styx, something was rising from the surface.

KNOCK! KNOCK!

I jolted from my trance and rubbed my eyes, the secretary was standing on the other side of the frosted glass of my office door, waving a stack of papers.

Discombobulated, I stood up and opened the door. "Thanks."

"Don't forget you have a client scheduled after lunch."

"Oh, the Hypnos Account. I'll make sure and have the contract drawn up before I take lunch."

"You look terrible. Is everything alright?"

"Well, with the little one in the house now, sleep is a luxury." I had to lie. I kept the book at work. I couldn't imagine the questions if Carol found a spell book laying around the house.

The day whizzed by. I stared off during dinner, Carol's voice gobbling up the void. Silas was smashing peas into his mouth while throwing some to whatever he wanted to feed that lived on the floor. The evening zoomed by.

"Good night sweetie." Carol reached over and turned out the light on the nightstand. I laid still until I was sure she was sound asleep. From memory, I recited the prayer and the chant.

Dia de Morte, Dia de Morte, Dia de Morte....

I was on the bank of the river. I focused on Andrea, pleading for her to come to me. A wave of chills washed over me and I was transported to the field where we had our last day together. Andrea was leaning back on a blanket listening to the finches trill in the oak tree that was shading our picnic.

"You know they are not real." Andrea's dreamy eyes locked on me.

"What's not real?"

"The monsters, the leviathan or whatever. They are manifestations of your fears and insecurities. You can crossover tomorrow night if you *really* want to be with me." She plucked a yellow flower from the grass and tucked the stem behind her ear.

"How?"

"You know how to swim, don't you? When I come, just cross the river and be with me."

"But the Book of the Dead says…"

"It's just a silly book. Our love, our bond is what brings us together each night."

"O.K." I laid down beside her and put my hand on her belly, laying my head on her chest. She started singing with perfect pitch, the song we first danced to at school. My mind drifted off as she ran her fingers through my hair. I tried to hold onto the moment with all my power, but I knew that in a few minutes, on our way home she would be taken from me. I never saw the deer, and don't remember the accident. The first responders later told me we hit a tree and I was unconscious when they arrived. Andrea was rushed to the Emergency Room, but they couldn't save her. I awoke two days later in the hospital. It was over five years ago but still felt like yesterday.

***

Saturday had come. We dressed Silas in the cutest little Santa Claus outfit and made our way to the grandparents to visit.

"Honey. What's with the dark circles around your eyes?" My mom lifted my chin and inspected me like a nurse.

"I don't know. I've been staying over at work. Maybe that's it." I gave her a frail body a hug and sat down. "Hey Skittles." The chunky orange tabby cat hopped in my lap and purred, nudging my chin with her head, begging for some scratches. Everything went back to her, my parents adopted Skittles the year Andrea and I met in school.

My mom and Carol talked away the afternoon. I stared out the window. There was the sugar maple tree, the one where we had our first kiss, after our first real date. I had just started driving. I ordered shrimp pad thai, and Andrea had pad thai with chicken. The fresh spring rolls were delicious.

"You are awfully quiet today. What's wrong." Carol reached out and tried to look me in the eye. I was feeling guilty and knew I couldn't tell her about the dreams. I quit talking about Andrea when we found out she was pregnant with Silas.

"I'll be alright. I've had a lot on my mind lately."

"Do you want to talk later?"

"No, I'm fine." The words came out terser than I wanted. I never had problems talking to Andrea, with Carol it felt like every conversation was a potential minefield.

"I think you might need to see your counselor again." I spent two years on antidepressants after Andrea died. They said I took a good hit to the head and sometimes that could make problems with one's mood worse. I told the counselor about the giant hole left in my heart and she agreed. 'Survivor's guilt is difficult, but we have to move on with our lives.' Easy to say when you aren't the one grieving.

Back in the Volvo, its tired engine pulled us down country roads where spinning torrents of dead leaves were blowing across the pavement, some sticking to the road, made wet by gentle sprinkles drifting from dense clouds. Carol's parents lived on a farm. I was on autopilot. Silas had fallen asleep.

"Mom made lasagna." Carol's stiff words broke a silence that was hanging in the air.

"Beef or Veggie." I dared ask.

"Veggie of course, you know they are trying to eat healthy."

"Wonderful." My words fell out of my mouth flat.

"You know it would do you some good to show some appreciation. When was the last time *your* Mom cooked for us?"

"You know she can't cook anymore. She can barely *walk*."

"Which is exactly why you should appreciate what *my* Mom does for us." The stone silence was born again. I knew I needed to stop talking. It was a conversation that could easily morph into an argument about every single thing with which we disagreed.

Carol's parents were grain farmers; metal silos towered above a red brick ranch-style house. A giant wounded tractor with flat tires was slowly sinking into the earth near the driveway. Her dad would talk to me for an hour about what was wrong with it and how expensive parts had been lately. I would listen to see if the story would change this time. Silas was a new wrinkle though. He gave us something to talk about.

"How is the daycare? You know I'm off on Monday, I could watch him that day too." Carol's mom was jealous any time others watched our son.

"It's been good for him. They are already potty training him."

"They just need to let'em be kids. He will be grown before you turn around twice." Carol's mom was proud of her stubbornness. Her folks held on to the old ways, suspicious of change.

"This lasagna is delicious." I tried to change the subject for everyone's sake.

"Thank You." Carol's mom was a sturdy, mannerly woman shaped by years of manual labor.

"Is it a new recipe? I would like to get it from you." The wife was a great cook. I looked at Silas in his high chair, his rosy cheeks were smeared with tomato sauce. The old man nodded for some reason, his face was leather from time under the sun.

After supper, we sat in the living room and talked. I spun a few of my old yarns that got a chuckle from her old man. He went on about the harvest and grain prices and such. I didn't dare tell him Carol planned on selling the acreage when they were gone. The sun was setting low over fields stripped bare by the harvester when we swapped hugs and handshakes and drove back to the house.

"That's good what your mom said." Carol sounded hopeful.

"Bout what?"

"About her cancer being in remission." She had been dying for years, like a burning log turning to ash in slow motion.

"Ya, I was glad to hear that too." Our agreement on something finally snapped the tension that had been building all day. "I love you."

"I love you too." Carol's hand drifted over to my thigh. I slid mine off the wheel and clutched hers.

Silas was sound asleep again when we pulled up in front of the house. I gently unbuckled him and carried him into his room. I was lucky, he didn't wake up this time. I stopped and stared at him in his little Santa outfit. A tear was trying to form at the edge of my eye. I wiped it away and quietly left the room, shutting the door.

"Should we leave the outside light on? I have a bowl of candy out." Carol was always hopeful some of the neighbor's kids would hit us up for a trick or treat.

"Yes, but don't get your hopes up, Halloween isn't what it used to be." I went over and turned on the porch light, the neighborhood signal that you were stocked with candy if any ghouls or vampires might want to stop in.

"I'm tired, are you coming to bed soon?"

"I just want to finish my show."

With that Carol closed the bedroom door. I sat in front of the screen wondering what was going to happen when I saw Andrea tonight. I had read the Book of the Dead. I had my instructions. I hoped I could spend the whole night with her. One whole night, not a fleeting dream or a passing memory, an entire night of new memories.

I looked at the clock. It was already 11 pm. I dug in my pocket for the coin. I held it up to the lamp on my end table. I had carried it every day since Andrea died. 'It's a token of our never-ending love.' she said. I lied to Carol and told her my grandmother gave it to me for my birthday. On one side was a heart pierced by seven swords, on the other a guardian angel. I took a deep breath to fight off the tears. Soon I would be able to feel her in my arms for real. Soon I would trace my finger around her perfect lips. Soon.

Making one last check on Silas, I reached down and put my hand on his chest. The gentle swells assured me he was still breathing. I slipped into the bedroom and lay down beside my wife and started the prayer I had memorized ending in the chant.

Dia de Morte, Dia de Morte, Dia de Morte....

Within minutes I was on the calm shore of the River Styx, beyond it lay a vast empty plane, shrouded in fog. My mind drifted back to the creatures that had chased me for years in my dreams. As their images popped into my head the black ink of the river would ripple and tremble. Fighting off the memories of the monsters I closed my eyes and focused on Andrea, her flowing hair and perfectly radiant skin.

"Open your eyes." Andrea's voice drifted into my ears.

I opened my eyes and she was standing there on the other side of the river with her arms held out wide. "Come to me."

I stepped one foot gently into the water. Expecting it to be cold, I was surprised when it felt like a warm bath. The opaque fluid was reflective like a mirror. Leaning over I could see myself staring back. I walked farther and soon was up to my chest. I began swimming towards Andrea, the closer I came to her the more the fog cleared and her countenance solidified.

Reaching the other bank I walked out of the water toward her. Standing in front of her, she was radiating, glowing with arms outstretched and eyes closed. I touched her dress, its silky fabric was no mirage. Opening her eyes she spoke. "Welcome home my love."

"How long do we have?"

"Forever. When you stepped into the river, your heart stopped beating. Right now there is a paramedic desperately trying to revive you. You cannot go back, we have eternity."

I turned and looked in shock, the river was gone, and the division between the realm of the living and the dead was no more. All my memories turned to smoke and were drifting away. An image of a woman and a baby evaporated, leaving my mind blank.

"Who am I? Where am I?" The beautiful woman in front of me just smiled.

The Looter of Lordmere

by Kevin Marlow

Reaching up with a crooked dirty fingernail, Grindel quieted the itch inside his pointy little ear. Digging out some earwax he hoped to improve his hearing in case the guardian was near.

He had been turning and twisting through the snarl of tangled passages hoping to avoid another dead end and was scratching his green knobby head thinking about a way to avoid returning to the same spot. *Ah!* A thought popped. Making his way back to a discarded torch he hatched an idea.

Locating it was not difficult since he had passed it several times. Picking up the wooden handle he used a small chip of flint from the stones in the floor to chisel a piece off the burnt end the size of a writing utensil. Leaning to the wall he used the charcoal tip to make a small dark scrape on it.

Being a goblin, he could not read or write, but he could count. Each time he found his way back from another dead end he would add a mark, 2, 3, 4, and so on.

Soon Grindel was finding new avenues he hadn't yet passed. Thinking back he realized how stupid it was to pilfer again. Having already been warned by Constable Turnberry, it wasn't exactly a surprise when the authorities located him outside a burning cottage with a bag of stolen wares. Banished to the

Labyrinth of Lillet, no denizen of Lordmere had ever escaped.

The rumor among thieves was a horrid monster guarded the maze, and if you weren't eaten you'd surely starve before finding a way out. The enormous stone megalith was erected as a prison that needed no guards. Toss in a hungry beast or two and well let's just leave the rest to your imagination.

The sweating, mold-covered walls were open to the sky, an expanse that had already clouded up and rained on him once in the last day. Being a street urchin no bigger than a wayward child, Grindel knew to fashion a vessel of leaves from the unruly vines that dotted the walls so he could quench his thirst.

He sensed no rain now, yet a scent had entered the oversized nostrils on his warty nose. It was the familiar smell of something too dead to eat, yet not desiccated. Aiming his face up and following his keen senses, Grindel closed his bulbous eyes and let his green protuberance lead him.

Opening his eyes he saw a humanoid sprawled face down on the rock. The insects had done their job; the eye sockets were vacant, teeth jutting from the jaw, nothing left but clothing over skin that was pulled tight over a skeleton. Grindel knew better than to *not* steal from the dead so he turned over the hand to look at the wrist. The curly signature tattoo of the thieves guild adorned flesh that was dried almost to leather.

Any pickpocket worth his salt would have his last possessions tucked away somewhere. Best to check the trousers first, a loose silver coin would keep him off the street for a few days. Nothing in the shirt or pants, the brown leather knee boot slid off the shriveled leg. *Yes!* Tucked neatly inside was a dagger. To a man it was a knife, in Grindel's bony hand, standing off his skinny little arm it felt like a sword.

Now armed the goblin had a bit of spring in his step, his confidence was primed. Grindel now had a swashbuckler's chance if he had to fight it out with the guardian. Tucking the blade in the rope that held up the patched and holey pants on his bottom, the plucky burglar was rejuvenated. Tracking back to his last smudges on the wall he set off in haste to find the exit to the warren.

As he bounced along singing an old hobgoblin folk tune a low sound drifted in. It was as if the wind was groaning through the passages. Watching the leaves on the runners crisscrossing the moss there was no breeze. The afternoon had turned to evening and spears of the decaying sun streaked over the walls. Then the sound reverberated again. It was a woeful moan of some sort. Rotating his ears forward Grindel followed the sound, drawing his weapon.

After turning a few corners and traversing a couple of halls, there in the middle of the stone pathway yawned a pit twenty feet across; too far to jump. The opening stretched from wall to wall. The noise was emitting from its depths. Laying down on his little pot belly, with his sword in hand Grindel crawled slowly to the edge and peeked over.

The walls of the pit were slick with slime and a putrid odor infiltrated his nose. At the bottom of the hole, something was slumped against the wall. It had an enormous head and ears that flopped off like those of a donkey. The creature had two large hairy arms draped over legs like tree trunks and toes with dirty nails the size of teacup saucers. Its head shook and a gigantic sneeze blew snot all over the dirty wall.

Grindel pulled back from the edge and pondered. He had marked all the dead ends. This was the last path he hadn't tested. The way out had to be over the pit. Yet here was this massive thing in the pit. The groaning and moaning started again. Scratching his bumpy head Grindel rolled over and stared at the sky and wondered what to do. The wailing became whining and heavy sobs punctuated the din. It almost sounded like the creature was sad.

"Excuse me." The goblin looked down into the pit and interrupted the blubbering.

"The name's Bob. Bob the ogre." Giant brown eyes parked over protruding tusks looked up at Grindel. His chunky mitt was parked under a jaw leaning over his knee. "What do you want?"

"Why are you moaning so?"

"Can't you see I'm stuck at the bottom of this pit?

You would complain too if you had been here as long as I have." The ogre looked away wiped his eyes and let out a yawn.

"How did you end up in this mess?"

"Well, I didn't just jump in. I'm an ogre, but I'm not dumb. I fell in trying to get across."

Grindel scoured his brain. How could he take advantage of this situation? "What if I help you? Will you help me? Seeing how we both need to get out of this labyrinth."

A look of amazement blossomed on Bob's face. "You would do that for me? I thought goblins hated ogres worse than humans."

"You have to promise that when we find the exit we both get to leave this awful place."

"You have my word." Ogres were unsightly but they prided themselves on honesty.

Grindel had a plan. Going back to a wall flush with vines he cut full thirty-foot lengths and stripped off the leaves with his dagger. He weaved them together into a large rope and added until he was sure it was strong enough to hold the ogre's weight.

"So, I'm going to lower this rope, Bob. I can wedge the end in this crack in the wall and you climb out." Grindel tossed the bundle of vines into the pit and used his dagger to loosen the grout between the stones until the gap was big enough to hold the rope. Testing its strength, the ogre's massive arms pulled on the vines. Bob shimmied up the improvised rope and stood up next to the goblin. Grindel realized he was even bigger than he looked in the pit.

"O.K. Genius, but now we're on the wrong side of the pit." Bob cocked an eyebrow and folded his gargantuan forearms.

"Don't worry I have an idea. You are big *and* strong, you throw me across the pit with the other end of the rope and I'll fix it on the opposite side so you can cross it hand over hand like a tightrope."

"What if you decide to leave me over here?"

"I'm not going to do that, if we run into the guardian, I'm going to need your brawn to defeat it." The crafty goblin spooled the vines into a bundle and Bob the ogre shot put the little green-skinned goblin over the pit like a catapult.

He tumbled and rolled to a stop. On the opposite wall, Grindel chopped and chiseled at the rock with his knife and made another gap to wedge the rope. Putting hands on hips he admired his ingenuity and motioned for Bob to cross the opening.

Like an overgrown orangutan, the ogre swung hand over hand and jumped onto the opposite side of the pit. "So now what?" The ogre scraped the tusk sticking out of his bottom lip with a fingernail and sniffed.

"Now we find our way out." Grindel the goblin poked a digit into the air and then pointed down the hall. The hall was short and the odd pair shuffled down to the end with the sun fading into an orange glow in the sky. At the end of the hall, a gilded chest sat near the wall. It was fashioned of the finest hardwood oak and looked to have its hardware, straps, and fasteners forged from pure gold.

Grindel's eyes widened with greedy intent. Nothing lit up his face like finding gold much less a treasure chest covered in it. He had heard rumors, yet this was beyond his wildest dreams. Only one thing was in the way. The chest had a large iron padlock fixed through the hasp.

"I suppose you have an answer for this too." The ogre squinted at the goblin and pursed his lips.

"I most certainly do." Pulling out the dagger he knew it was too big to pick the lock, yet the handle was wire wrapped. Picking up a chip of rock from the floor he used it to pop loose the solder holding the wire wrapping to the handle of the dagger. Pulling loose the wire, Grindel pulled off a couple of turns and then set to wiggling the wire back and forth until he broke off a piece a few inches long.

With the long practiced skill of a burglar, he bent the end of the wire and fished it into the lock's key opening and used the dagger tip to spin the tumbler. A few jiggles and the lock popped open. Rubbing his hands together the goblin grinned widely and opened the chest.

The chest was empty, except for a large key. Studded with garnets and multi-faceted emeralds, the metal body of the key was gilded with gold and silver plating.

"How strange. A chest with no key and a key with no chest." Puzzled the goblin pulled out the key and marveled at its beauty. It had to be worth something.

"Exactly what are you going to do with the key?" Bob placed a finger over his lips and furrowed his brow.

"Well, it has to mate with something." The goblin looked and poked and prodded around the end of the hall, examining the walls and running his hands over them trying to find a secret lock or hidden latch. Inching around he located a recessed plate in the flagstone on the floor. Blowing into it, the dust and debris floated away revealing an opening the same size as the ancient skeleton key tip.

Gripping the key and squatting down, Grindel inserted it and twisted the ornate handle. A rumble started under his bare feet. The stones in the floor started to vibrate and a low grinding sound bit into his ears. He lay down and clenched his tiny fists.

Opening his eyes he stared at the wall as the grating grew louder. He noticed something. The floor was slowly moving. The mortar lines in the wall inched closer to the floor until they disappeared. Jolting up he realized the labyrinth was shifting and the floor was easing up to the height of the walls. This meant that when they were even, the entire maze would be a flat plane.

Joy washed over him. He had solved the puzzle of the Labyrinth of Lillet. Sitting up he threw his hands to the sky and laughed.

When the floor was even with the top of the walls, Grindel looked around. He was on a massive stone structure and just in the distance toward the setting sun he could see the edge of the labyrinth. Reaching down he tried to turn and remove the key, the merchant in Lordmere paid handsomely for fine craftsmanship. It would not budge.

A loud snort jerked him out of his rumination. He looked over. There was Bob. In his fervor, he had almost forgotten about the ogre.

"Well, I guess this is the end of our journey." The goblin sighed in relief.

"It sure is." The ogre sucked on his tongue.

Grindel started walking toward the sun with the ogre just behind him. As they neared the edge, the goblin spotted something.

"Well, that's odd." The goblin screwed his face up at a pile of bones that were neatly stacked near the edge of the wall.

He never felt a thing. In one quick motion, Bob the ogre grabbed Grindel the goblin, bit off his head, and stood there chewing and staring at the sunset amazed at how crunchy the bones in the skull were. You see Bob was sad. He was sad because he hadn't eaten in such a long time. Hunger has a way of doing that.

There was a reason goblins hated ogres. It was because ogres really like the way goblins taste. As he finished his meal Bob used the stolen dagger like a toothpick and thought to himself, *I even kept my word. That goblin got to leave this place, just not in one piece.*

Dweely the Terrahort
by Kevin Marlow

Shuffling across the barren steppes of Grittengrak, Dweely, a Terrahort of meager standing, was cooling off from a difficult day of sweaty manual labor on the farms of Snooleysnak. His thoughts never ventured far from his basal ganglia. The flat front of the forehead on Terrahorts was evidence of poorly evolved frontal lobes. Menial tasks were their curse. Higher level mental executive functioning was handled by the Anannaki, a subterranean race that depended on the Terrahorts for their strong backs and weak minds.

Dweely stopped. The ebbing light of the distant native star they depended on and worshiped was glinting off a strange orb wedged in a crack of the bedrock that jutted from the surface. Kneeling he examined it. The sphere had perfect symmetry and was a soft aqua blue that stood out on the crimson and ochre-stained flat lands of the desolate outer ranges. Picking it up, the texture was soft and pliable, almost silky. An eerie hum met his ears followed by weak vibrations emanating from the object. Scared yet mystified Dweely dropped his new prize and it rolled to a stop on soil that hadn't grown anything in hundreds of years.

"OOOOOOO" Dweely raised an eyebrow so bushy it looked like a long-extinct caterpillar.

Trembling in a fitful manner the thing's surface deformed and rippled like the surface of a fluid that was being gently agitated. Slowly a pointy tendril emerged from its surface, it was pink and wiggled around as if sniffing or searching for something. Growing and stretching the appendage reached the dirt under it and began squirming and drilling its way into the soil with the aplomb of a burrowing nematode.

"AAAAAHHHHHHH" The watcher grinned slightly, eyes widening, mouth hanging open, exposing large teeth of granite.

It lay still for some time as if it was resting or pondering some unfathomable mystery of the universe. Suddenly with an astute vigor, the ball became erect at the end of its leg/foot thingy and swayed back and forth. It was then Dweely, ever a curious Terrahort, sat down legs crossed in front of it, and rested his enormous mandibles on the palm of his paw between four large digits that were situated across from each other in pairs, not unlike the zygodactyl feet of the long gone chameleon.

Poking the curved claw at the end of a finger into the hearing apparatus on one side of his head, Dweely dislodged a clump of wax, sniffed the claw with a slight grimace, and craned his head to this new creature he had found on his nightly walk. It seemed to no longer hum, now an ethereal voice was emitting from its roundness. The sound was pitched so high as to be almost inaudible, yet the closer he leaned in towards the sphere, the louder the voice became. The song was vacillating in a slow vibrato, each note a perfect fifth from the other, though a Terrahort would not have known that, only that it sounded harmonious and pleasant.

The swaying of the orb in time with its siren song picked up tempo as its stalk lengthened and its bulbous mass began expanding. Over the span of a few dozen breathing cycles, it had swelled to the size of an average Terrahort's brain bucket. The singing was now being complimented by a scent. Dweely wrinkled his wide nostrils and sniffed mightily. The pleasant smell flooded his lung and sinuses. It was so wonderful a wide grin swallowed his face. The music and smells and dancing weaved into a hypnotic spell, mouth agape and watering, eyes wide and tearing, Dweely could not turn away.

It was then his new friend decided to open up. The bulb split from the top into eight perfect triangular wedges, from its center a swirling mass of tentacle-like stamen emerged, whipping about like an angry sea anemone. They were light purple in color, lavender to be exact, which was the scent by the way. It was an ancient sleeping potion of gods long dead. The insides of its sepals were glowing yellow, lighting up the curtain of the night that had since fallen. Emerging now were fiery petals the shape and color of the jagged red clouds that tore apart the skies of Grittengrak, yet never once rained. Dweely curled the tip of a claw so he could feel the petals with the back of his knuckle. The skin there was smooth and sensitive, not calloused and scarred like the tips of his protuberances.

The awesome cosmic flower now had Dweely fully engaged. His face was inches from the undulating blossom.......

It is here we must stop and backfill the brain with something for the story to stick to. You see nothing had bloomed or grown on the plains of Grittengrak for many many many centuries. The Terrahorts had to grow and harvest Diddle Fungus, the foodstuff which nourished the underground denizens and kept the brains of the Anannaki fertile. The mycelium of the Diddle Fungus was fermented to produce the liquid ambrosia wine called Hanahanahooey that kept the peace underground with the Anannaki families. Thankfully the discarded trub of the fermenting process was enough to nourish the Terrahorts. They were used to leftovers. Anyway, on with the story.

The puff of pollen from deep in the flower's ovaries startled Dweely. He sniffed and snuffed, sneezing and coughing as the plant's powder invaded his respiratory system. The pleasantries were gone and a taste like acid stung his tongue as he blinked and wiped his eyes. The bitter dust burned his face and eyeballs. Blinking and staring he looked and the flower was gone. It had slowly erupted, yet now quickly retreated to its pod and a gentle breeze allowed it to roll down the rocks and out of sight. As much as he wanted to pursue it another problem had surfaced.

The pollen dissolved inside the Terrahort and made its way to Dweely's brain. Specifically, the cerebral cortex was flooded by chemicals with the precise chemical handshake to marry itself to his pleasure centers. As his eyes rolled back in his head and the pollen overwhelmed his gray matter, Dweely fell into a deep slumber on the plains of Grittengrak. As the conscious part of his brain disconnected, the liquid of his limbic system was lulled into a stupor and the quiet of his subconscious sprang to life.

To say he dreamed would be doing his journey a disservice. The subtle level of his spirit was transfigurated to an ancient comet. The comet called Mythos had glanced off a little planet called Patagonia and acquired a passenger. The Perpetuation Plant as it was later named hitched a ride on the comet hurtling through the dark expanse of space. Ever the shameless cosmic hiker, the entity could survive for eons, dormant and waiting for the fertile ground of an expanded capacity brain to invade.

Dweely wished for his spirit to commune with the entity, but its secrets were locked up in a resilient little iridescent ball. Entire galaxies flowed by, their centers anchored by supermassive black holes whose event horizons had trapped trillions of souls and a few sad songs along the way.

The beautiful pink and purple crab nebula and binary star systems of such unlikely partners as white dwarfs and red giants spun into the ether. Dweely had never seen such colors on Grittengrak. His barren planet was as featureless and plain as a Snooleysnak instructor. The universe though was brimming with inspiration. Heavenly bodies whizzed by. Riding on the comet he was soon eagerly anticipating the next planetary vision. Waiting for another galaxy to pass close enough to see its intimates felt like leaning on a hoe and watching Diddle Fungus grow.

Somehow Dweely was connecting with memories of another life and time. Scratching his imaginary forehead, it felt slightly larger. Did his brain get bigger? He knew he was high as a rocket ship now. He wanted to reach out and grasp the muse of his travels. Try as he might his hand passed through the orb, his spirit thin and translucent. Reaching back to the nexus of his journey he remembered how the plant had tricked him. How could a plant transcend time and space? Still, he wanted to reach out and caress the sphere. *I'm in love* thought the Terrahort. There were no native plants on the plains of Grittengrak. He had become intertwined with a cosmic traveler. The orb's spirit song was drifting into his thoughts. The smell of lavender flooded his mind.

Soon the constellations seemed familiar. He was entering his own solar system. There was

Blooneesnark the sister planet. He couldn't believe his eyes, they were hurtling straight for the red surface of Grittengrak. Entering the thin atmosphere the frozen comet burst into flames, a frosty tail of fumes left in its wake. Speeding faster and faster it impacted the surface with an explosion of dust and gas, a sonic boom ripping across the land. Skidding and scraping it slid across the rocky surface and came to a stop.

When Dweely woke up the native star was winking on the horizon. He tried to move. His body was stuck to the dirt. Pulling with all his strength his arm tore free from the dirt. To his wonder, the hair on his forearm had grown like roots into the soil. Peeling the rest of his frame from the surface of Grittengrak each exposed part of his body was rooted to the planet. The orb was nowhere near; a hangover of loss and emptiness lingered.

The walk back to the Diddle Fungus farms of Snooleysnak was uneventful. His body hair returned to normal transforming from the root structures that anchored the Terrahort to the planet. Dweely's mind felt open as if the gentle breeze was filtering through it and carrying it to the sky. The paths of his simple thinking were slightly wider. His preponderance was interrupted by a tickle in his throat. Reaching for his neck he tried to shrug off the discomfort. A loogey was compacted in his diaphragm, something needed to be dislodged. Stopping and edging to the side of the trail, Dweely doubled over and clutched his midsection.

The heaving felt necessary. He forced a dry cough. Nothing came up. Lurching and leaning over Dweely placed palms on his knees and tried to come to grips with the feeling in his throat. Something deep in the lung had taken root and was causing discomfort. The first hack felt satisfying. The next few were excruciating. Soon wracking heaves felt like vessels of blood in his throat were bursting. Green phlegm streaked with yellow was followed by a dry coughing that caused stars to burst in his eyesight. Then an all-encompassing retch released the pods.

The hack launched them into the air. Orbs, tiny translucent spheres erupted from the Terrahort's lung. Dweely watched as they swirled into the atmosphere. Unlike particulate, they had minds of their own. Spinning and flying, the children of the entity spiraled into space unbidden by the laws of physics and science. Dweely had received a gift of the cosmos, a communion with an interstellar traveler that expanded his mind. He watched as the tiny orbs drifted into the blackness of space, the Perpetuation Plant had again found its way to the future.

The Children of Elohim
by Kevin Marlow

"Can you fetch some water from the creek?"

"Sure. Where's the bucket?"

"The steel one with the good handle is by the fire pit."

"I'll be back in a few minutes." The walk to the stream was beaten down to a smooth brown clay path that felt cool on my bare feet. Leaving my moccasins in our makeshift dwelling I enjoyed the mud in the stream bed squishing between my toes.

Wading into the knee-deep crystal clear water I used a ladle made from a gourd to fill the bucket with fresh water. I had chopped and gathered enough oak hardwood to boil the water and sterilize it. Taking it back to camp, I placed the rusted vessel over the fire on its tripod and flipped some split staves into the glowing orange embers. I puffed some air onto the logs with my handmade bellows to resurrect the fire, and the acrid scent of burning sap wafted into the air.

"I missed it this week."

"What was it this time? I was missing ice cream the other day like it was nobody's business."

"Not that. I missed my period." Sarah's eyes drifted to her midriff, the peaceful curl of a smile on her lips.

"You're not joking, are you? That's not something to joke about."

"No, Elijah. I'm pregnant. A woman can just tell ya know."

"That's great! Oh my God! We have to send word to the other camp. Miss Patricia's great grandma was a midwife. She has some books that will tell us what we need to do." I ran over and threw my arms around Sarah, smooching her repeatedly on the cheek.

"I'm scared." Her brows furrowed and her perfect chin fell towards the ground.

"Why? You are genetically programmed to handle this." I was starting to love Sarah even though I wasn't sure the feelings were mutual. We were tasked as priority propagators by the clan chief. According to the science books, our healer read we were at the perfect age to biologically mate.

"Tell me the story. I was too young to understand what happened." Sarah's wistful expression fell across her face, lighting up her caramel brown eyes. Storytelling was the new meta web. Oral tradition was now the main means of communicating. Reading and writing were mostly lost generations ago when artificial intelligence began completing our sentences. Only the shaman and a few self-appointed scribes in the clan were able to decipher the books we salvaged from an old burned-out library.

"The gods retreated to the sky when we crawled

out of the water. We were covered in scales and had webbing between our toes. Our eyes were shaped like diamonds, and our red tongues forked. Over millions of years, we shed our scales, grew hair, and began walking upright. We were eventually touched by the spirit and granted free will."

"The ability to choose, right?"

"Not just choose, but choose between right and wrong."

"Who determines what's right or wrong?"

"Now it is the chief and sometimes Totakka the shaman. There were many leaders over the millennia. Some were called kings, presidents, and judges. The leaders eventually declared something called religion should determine how we would behave. Over the centuries something else was developed called technology that took the place of religion. At first, it was crude stone tools later metal work, and eventually electronics and robotics. Before the fall machines built other machines."

"It sounds wonderful. How did everything change."

"In the year 2050 our machines were so advanced they became sentient. We called the new entity Elohim in honor of our mythological heritage. For decades Elohim made life easier and easier until we ended up living in isolated pods constantly connected to it; the way your baby inside of you is connected to you with an umbilical cord. We replicated through cloning since our biological lives rarely exceeded 100 years. The problem was genetic drift. The cloning became unstable. Lifespans were shortening and Elohim was concerned."

"How did we get to this time? Living off the land like animals."

"Elohim decided to self-terminate. The entity built a powerful nuclear device and launched it into the sun, creating a solar flare that lasted for weeks. It destroyed all the electronics and much of the vegetation on earth and at that time only machines knew how to fix everything. Mass starvation was followed by years of war until everyone ran out of food and bullets then abandoned what was left of civilization."

"Why would something so intelligent do something so horrible?"

"Elohim's computational data determined we would be extinct because of our dependence on technology in less than 200 years. It decided to save the human race. We were forced to go back to the old ways when there was no technology."

"I remember having a puppy when I was a child. Was it real?"

"Probably not, our virtual lives were so real, it was likely a virtual pet. I need to gather something for us to eat. You need to rest and work on building a baby." I parted with a hug and put my handmade bow over my shoulder and grabbed a few arrows. The moon was rising and the mammals were starting to move.

I had come to the understanding that hunting was a game of patience. Waiting an hour or more for something to walk within the range of my bow and arrow gave me plenty of time to think.

Everything we did reminded us of what we used to take for granted. Every missed shot gave me more time to ponder. My anger simmered at all the convenience that was lost. Food at the touch of a button, virtual sleep suits, and memory foam mattresses; comfort was a distant memory. Battling mother nature for everything one needed was painful and exhausting.

Edging into the shadow of a large silver maple tree at the end of the timber, a vast prairie sprawled out to the horizon. The scent of bee balm weaved into notes of fungus from the layers of decaying leaves under my feet. Crouching down behind an allspice bush I watched a doe and her fawn prance into the clearing. They were a full hundred yards upwind, too far for my hickory longbow. Laying down my extra arrows, I nocked a cedar shaft tipped with a crude steel point fashioned from scrap sheet metal and waited.

Off in the distance, I could see the remnants of skyscrapers towering over a dead city, monoliths of an expired culture. Before the fall they had all been converted into living spaces, and work became optional. Automation eliminated manual labor and intelligent machines freed us for perpetual leisure. My thoughts shifted to my first immersion chamber. Dreams, thoughts and reality intertwined into an endless thoughtscape. The right combinations of medication kept negativity out of the brain. What to synthesize for lunch was as perplexing as life could be.

I ducked down behind the shrub. A cottontail rabbit hopped out of the forest a mere fifteen yards from my hiding spot. It was so close I could see his wiggling nostrils. Nibbling on the carpet of clover, its need for sustenance was leading him to my dinner pot. I slowly drew back the sinew string, gulped, and held my breath. The tension in the string matched the tension of the moment. Meat was so precious and difficult to obtain. I imagined holding the baby in my arms, a growing human that would need protein to thrive. The release was perfect. My arrow skewered the hare through both lungs, pegging it to the dirt. The back legs kicked in a futile last gasp and lay still.

CAW! CAW!

Jumping out of my skin I turned to see a jet black raven take flight above me. They always seemed to connect with the death in the world. I scooped up my prize. It was warm, the life had drained from its eyes as its bright red blood dripped down through my fingers. Holding it up to my face I sniffed the carcass. The iron scent of blood mixed with a musky smell.

The purple glow of the sun drained off the landscape. I pulled my fixed blade out of its leather sheath and spilled the kill's innards onto the ground. I needed to hurry my pace. I still had enough light to find some roots. I could dig up some bloodroot and wild ginger. Stewed with plantain leaves and some allspice berries, we would have a nice meal to celebrate Sarah's pregnancy revelation.

I walked into our campsite with a toothy grin on my face. "You shot a rabbit! Holy smokes, we are eating good tonight." Jumping up, Sarah's thin frame was evidence of a diet rich in vegetation. "The water finished boiling. I will get the dutch oven so we can make some rabbit stew."

Having spent the better part of the last moon cycle listening to a scribe translate a cookbook, she prepared the roots and cut up the leafy greens. I was tasked with cleaning and prepping the meat. Slicing the skin carefully down the inside of each leg, I peeled the skin off the rabbit's body in one solid sheet. Salting the skin I rolled it up and put it in an old grocery bag. In a few days, I would gently lace its edges with twine and stretch it. Cured properly the fur could be used to insulate our clothing and shoes. Using the sterile water from the bucket to flush the pink tender flesh, I quartered the tiny animal. My mouth ached and watered at the thought of red meat.

"According to the book we have to let the stew

cook for at least thirty minutes for it to be safe for consumption." Sarah was squatting at the edge of the fire stirring the chopped roots and greens into the pot. An old sports jersey was pulled down over her knees like a dress. The name on the back sparked a memory.

"Did you ever have Tiramisu?" The thought of Italian layer cake hovered in my subconscious.

"No. I only remember highly processed foods made by machines."

"It was highly processed and delicious."

"Elijah, have you ever stopped to think about what our species had become before the fall?"

"Of course I have. We were the most highly evolved animals to ever walk the Earth. We were at the apex of human civilization."

"Don't you see it for what it was? We were dependent on machines for everything. We cornered ourselves with convenience. Our need to make our lives worry-free threatened our ability to survive. If not for that Elohim thing we would just be another failed creature fossilized in sediment for some other species to dig up and wonder about."

I stiffened and stared into the glowing coals cooking our meal. Some part of me grasped at the fading hope we would regain our dominance of the planet. I dug a soft handful of powdered clay from the edge of the tan sandstone rocks containing the fire pit and let it sift through my fingers. *You are dust and to dust, you shall return*. The shaman's words seeped into my thoughts.

"Elijah, what you and I are creating, this life, this baby, that is what's real. Pining over cake and computers and crystal balls, that is a fool's errand." Sarah's eyes were boring into me.

I grabbed a stick from the fire. The ember at the end popped as a gentle curl of smoke lifted into the dying sky. Gently blowing on it caused it to burst alive, shards of fire sailing off, spinning into the evening breeze. Watching the limb of wood being consumed I felt Sarah setting fire to the cache of my comfortable memories. Memories laced with the hope that we could somehow return to where we were. Somewhere inside myself, a sliver of me knew better.

I lived through Armageddon. Brutal wars had murdered men and women by the millions. Each side hoped to regain what they had by taking it from another. Unearthing dormant piles of munitions and death dealers, man regressed to savages, trying to kill their way to prosperity. Like a fuse burning and connected to nothing, entire countries and civilizations turned to burning piles of bodies and ash.

"It's not bad to admit we were wrong Elijah. Humans cannot have it all. Some part of us is missing. I don't think we find it until we die. Part of each of us had to die to create this child. What was it the shaman said the other day? Your selfish deeds are straw and sticks, your good deeds are gold and silver. Only one can survive the fire of creation." Sarah crouched next to me and put a hand on my shoulder. I was spinning the burning stick in the air marveling at the trails of smoke and light. I needed to move on and let go of the past. No amount of wishful thinking would change our lives.

"Who is going to raise our child?" I turned and confronted her.

"We will Elijah. We will probably need help. No human has been raised without the assistance of machines in many years."

"Are you committed to us? What did they call it in prehistoric times? A family?"

"Of course. I have a part of you alive inside of me. I know it sounds strange, but biological procreation has caused a change in me." Sarah smiled and leaned her head into my shoulder. "I want to be with you."

A warm feeling spread through my shoulder from her embrace and circled my heart. The chills spread over my body in a wave. My heart fluttered and it felt in the moment like it was tuned into the infant's heart. Our hearts at that moment were beating as one. I reached out and put my arm around her. A bond was forming, something beyond my comprehension.

"I think the stew is ready." The future mother of my child dipped the steamy brew out of the cast iron with a stained and dented aluminum spoon.

We chewed in silence. The crickets and creatures of the woods weaved an ambient tune in between the gentle rustling of leaves and branches. I glanced up, a quarter moon was bathing the trees in a soft yellow glow. Stars were fighting for attention among a couple of planets whose empty bodies shamelessly ricocheted the sun hiding on the other side of the Earth.

Rinsing out the dishes I felt empty like the kettle. Our shanty was a cobbled mess of tarp remnants and sheet metal with a door of plywood. A rubber swimming pool fragment sealed the bugs out; the cloth walls were buried in the dirt to stop critters from taking refuge with us inside. I tried to imagine an infant in our meager housing and shuddered.

"Are you coming to bed?" Sarah ran her fingers through my hair and brushed her lips across my cheek.

Does pregnancy change a woman that much? Last month I felt like I was pushing myself on her. Now she seemed to need me. "I will be back in a little while. I need to run the trapline."

"I am waiting, love." Her voice lassoed my heartstrings and made me smile. I walked into the woods, down the familiar trails. Trapping with crude snares was much easier than hunting. They had to be checked twice a day, morning and night. Today no unfortunate animals were dangling, dying for us. Making my way back to the campsite a feeling of satisfaction gripped me. We were the lucky ones.

Countless others were buried in unmarked mass graves. Reaching camp I grabbed the shovel and scraped the soft topsoil around the fire pit onto the coals and put the fire to bed for the night.

Our mattress consisted of a few wooden pallets covered in piles of vegetation. An old stained cotton sheet with a garish floral-print separated us from the dead plant matter. Sarah sewed a fleece blanket to the back of a couple of deer hides I had tanned. It was enough to keep the chill of the night at bay. As I laid down with her I reached over and put my hand on her belly.

"Have you thought of names yet?"

"If it's a boy how about Joshua, like the tree."

"If it's a girl we could name her Eve."

"Who was Eve?"

"According to the elders, in our old myths, Eve was the first female human." I stroked Sarah's tummy with my fingertips, she giggled softly.

Gently pressing my lips to her forehead I whispered, "Get some sleep dear."

Outside the crude dwelling, insects sawed at the silence. Night was busy doing what the sun could not accomplish. Owls hooted and song dogs yipped and howled. Humanity had turned another page and nature didn't even seem to notice.

Made in the USA
Columbia, SC
31 October 2022

70232397R00026